KNITTING
WORSTED

A GIFT FROM
THE LONELY DOLL

DARE WRIGHT

Houghton Mifflin Company
Boston

To Florence Wakeman,

Edith's friend and mine

Copyright © 1966 by Dare Wright

All rights reserved. For information about permission to reproduce
selections from this book, write to Permissions, Houghton Mifflin
Company, 215 Park Avenue South, New York, New York 10003.

First published in New York by Random House, Inc.

www.houghtonmifflinbooks.com   *2562660*

Library of Congress Catalog Card Number: AC 66-10604
RNF ISBN 0-618-07181-4   PAP ISBN 0-618-07182-2

Manufactured in the United States of America

LBM 10 9 8 7 6 5 4 3 2 1

"Christmas is coming," said Edith.

"How soon?" asked Little Bear.

"In three weeks and four days," said Mr. Bear. "And we're all going to the country for the holidays."

"Where?" asked Edith.
"To visit my cousins, Charles and Albert," said Mr. Bear.

"How?" asked Little Bear.
"On a train," said Mr. Bear.
"When?" asked Edith.
"The week before Christmas," said Mr. Bear.

"We'd better start getting ready for Christmas, Little Bear," said Edith. "I'm going to knit Mr. Bear a fine, woolly muffler to wear in the country."

"I bet you don't know how to knit," said Little Bear.

"I do too, and a present you make is nicer than just a bought present," said Edith.

So Edith went shopping.

She bought two long knitting needles.

She bought a skein of yarn as white as snow.

She bought a skein of yarn as red as holly berries.

She made Little Bear help her wind the yarn.

"Now let's see you knit," said Little Bear.

"It's going to be a striped muffler," said Edith.

"Knit!" said Little Bear.

Edith surprised him. She did know how!

She knitted one row, and two rows, and three rows.

In no time she had knitted a whole inch of muffler.

Every day the muffler grew.

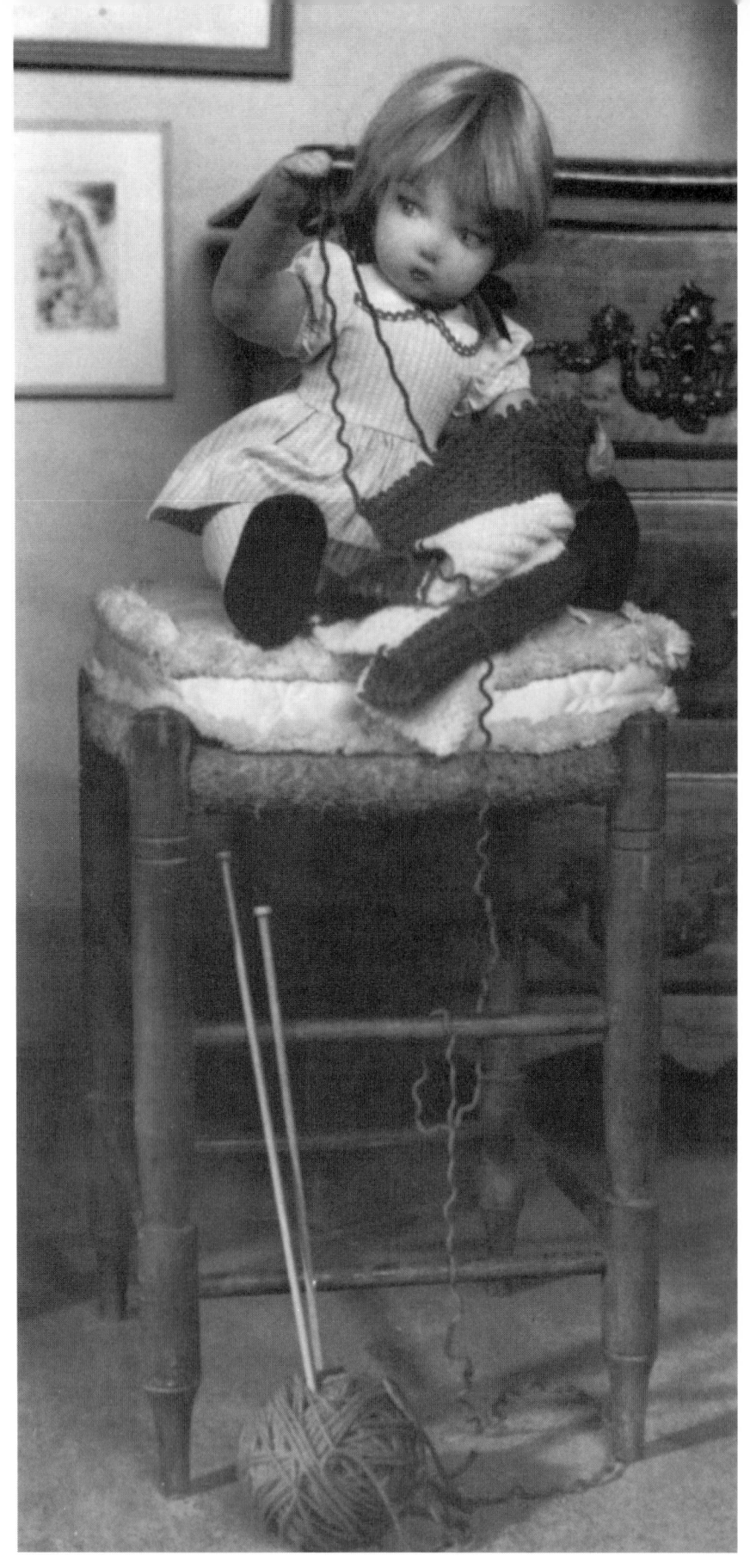

Except for the days when it ungrew!
One day Edith dropped a stitch, and had to unravel
a whole stripe.

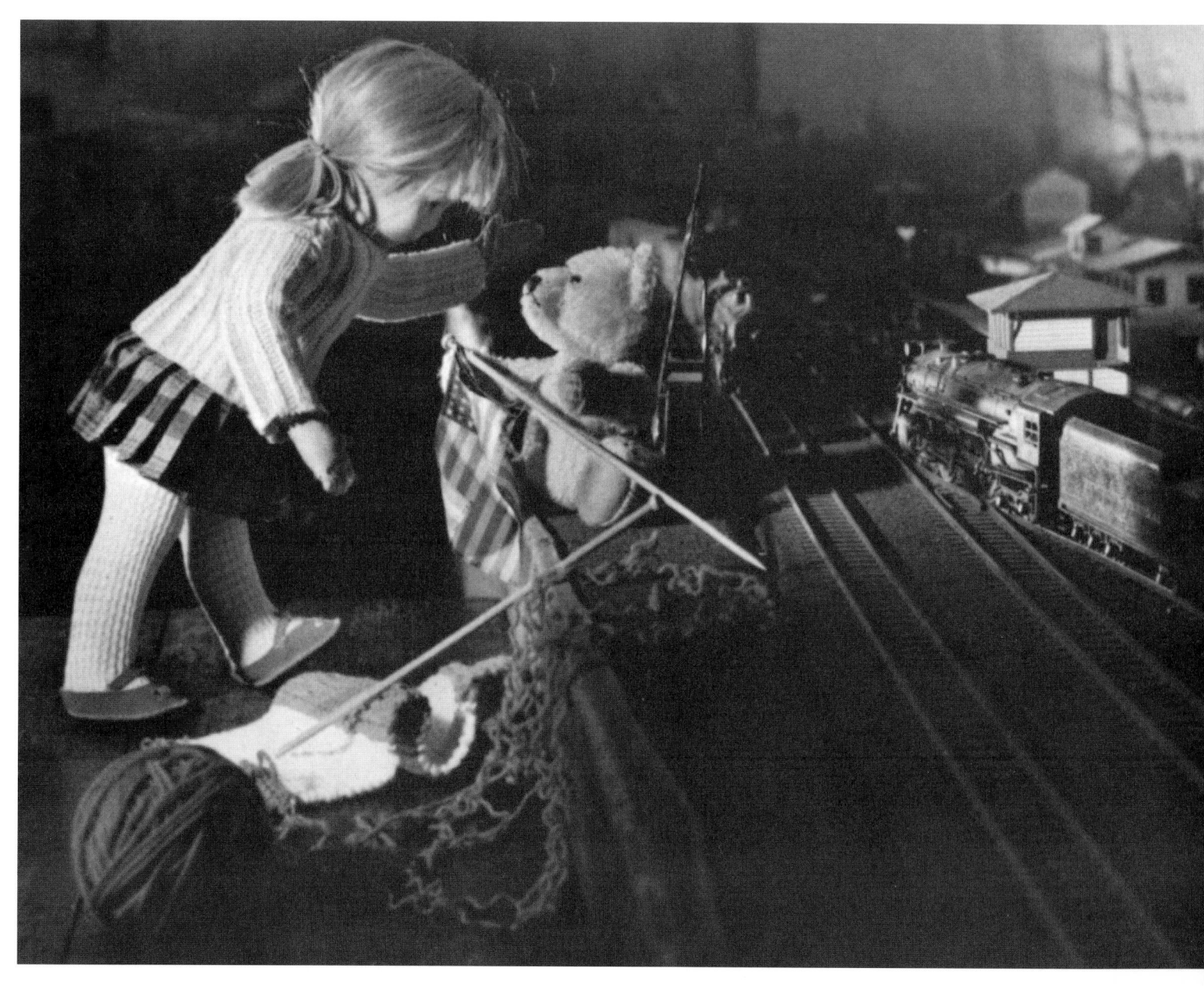

One day Little Bear borrowed her needles to make
flagpoles for his railway.
That unraveled another stripe.

Edith had a basket to keep her knitting hidden in—
all but the end she was working on.

Of course she could never knit when Mr. Bear was
anywhere around.

"Isn't that muffler ever going to get finished?" asked
Little Bear when two weeks had gone by.
"Of course," said Edith. "In time for Christmas."
"I bet you're making it too long," said Little Bear.

"I am not!" said Edith.

"Let's measure how long it is," urged Little Bear.

"Oh, no," objected Edith. "What if I took it all out of the basket at once and Mr. Bear walked in!"

Every time Mr. Bear was especially nice to her—

Edith knitted another stripe.

Every time she was especially naughty—

she knitted another stripe.

She wasn't finished when they left for the country.

"Do you have to take that basket along, Edith?"
inquired Mr. Bear.

"Yes, I do," said Edith.

Cousin Charles Bear and Cousin Albert Bear met
them at the station.
They looked so much like Mr. Bear that Edith loved
them on sight.

The house was warm and cozy.
The fields were deep in snow.
There were all kinds of things for
Edith and Little Bear to do.
They went sledding on the hills.

They skated on the ponds.

They chose their own Christmas tree in the woods.

On Christmas Eve they helped to trim it.
When the last ornament was in place —
"Off to bed, Edith and Little Bear," ordered the three
big bears. "We have secrets and surprises to arrange."

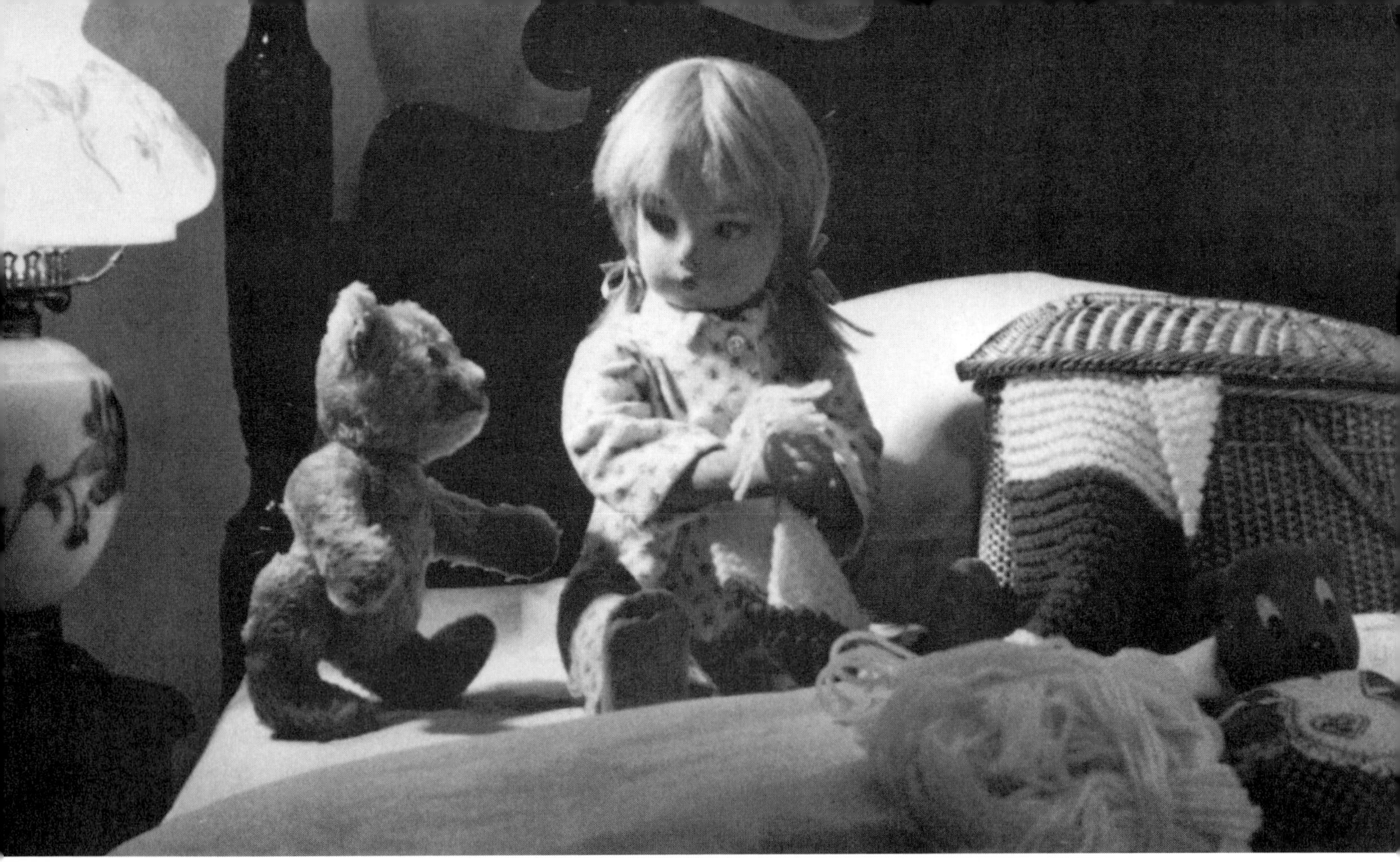

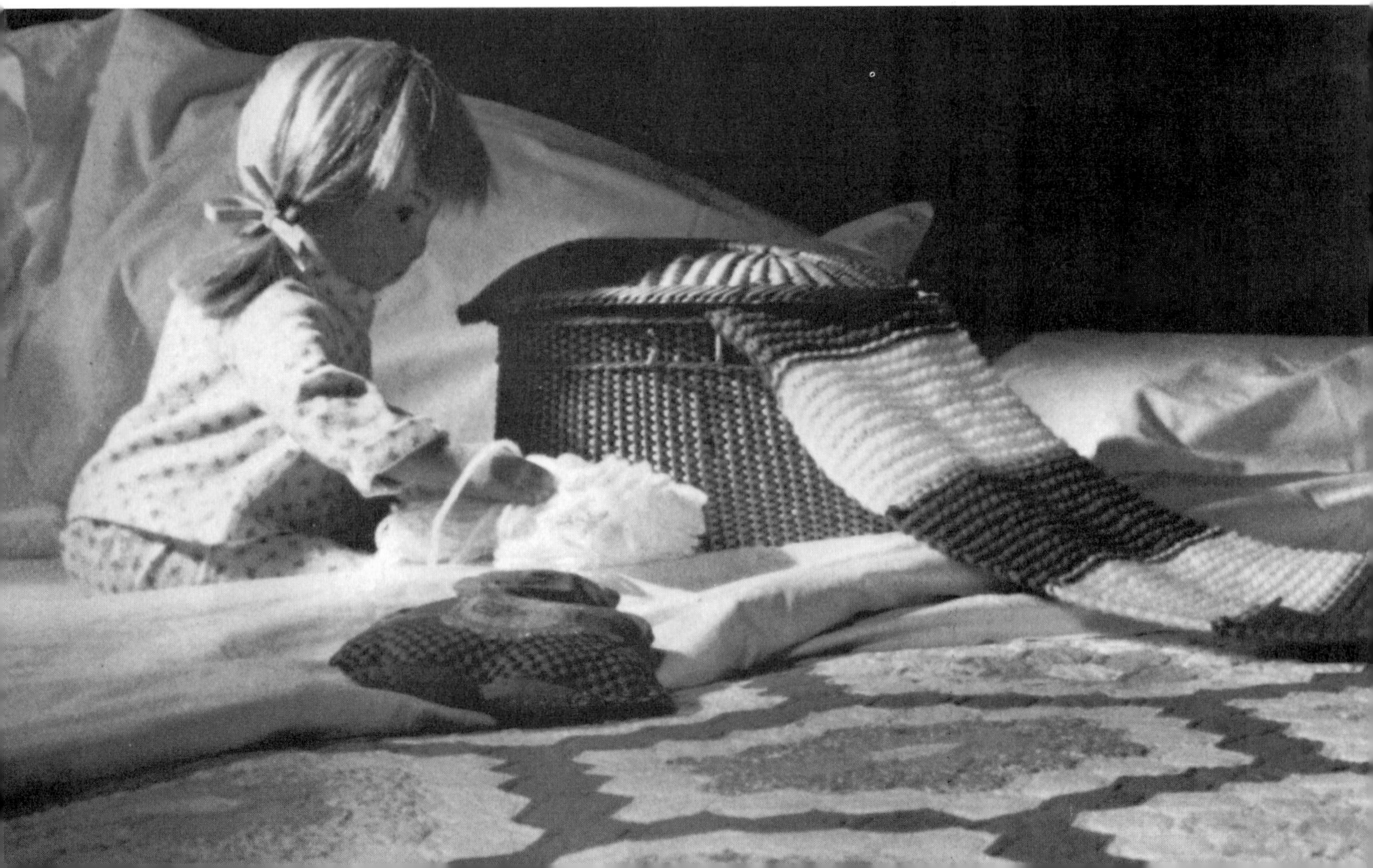

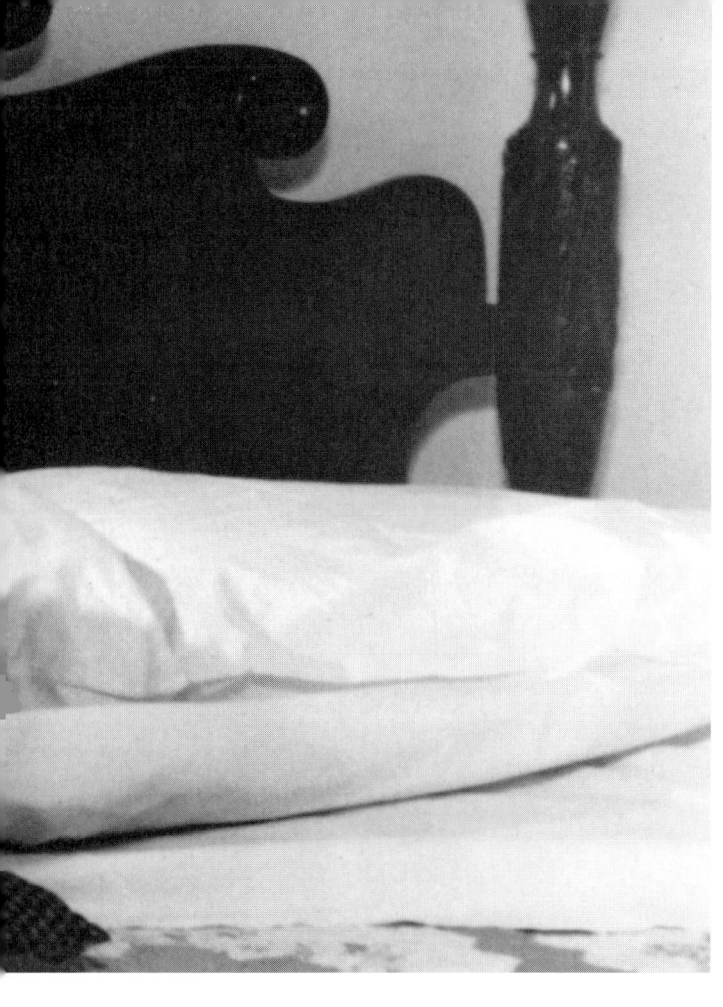

So Edith and Little Bear
went to bed, but they didn't
stay there.
"Is *that muffler* finished?"
demanded Little Bear.
"As soon as I put fringe on
the ends," said Edith.

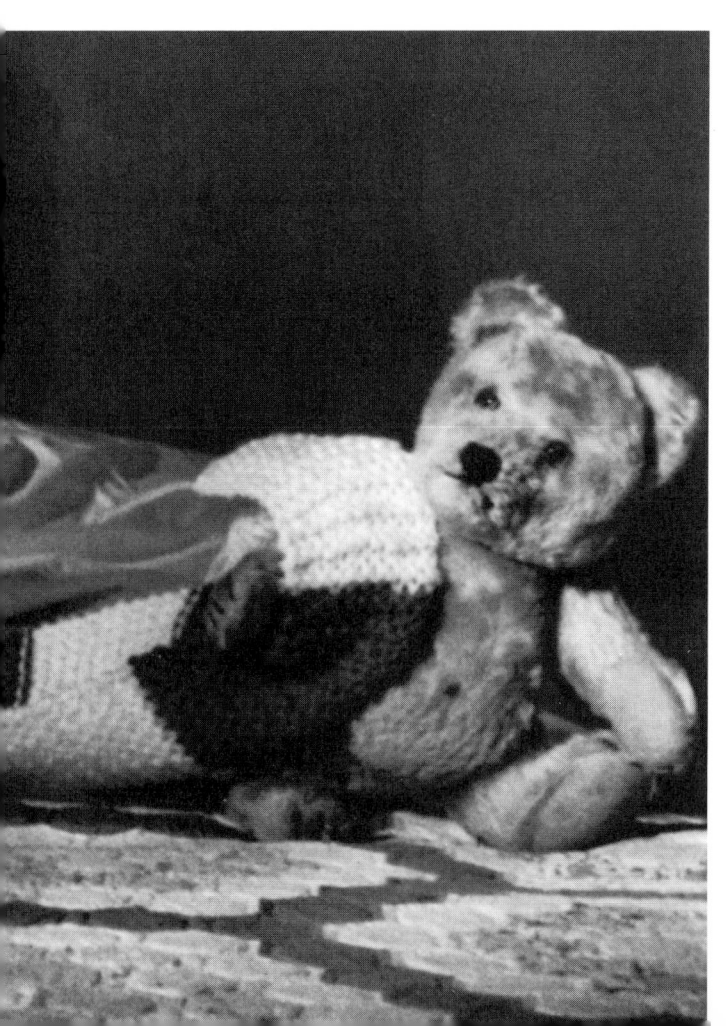

"I want to see all of it,"
insisted Little Bear.
He began pulling.
More and more muffler
came out of the basket.

It reached all across the room.

"Too long!" shouted Little Bear. "I told you so!"

"It is not too long!" said Edith stubbornly. "It's just long
enough to keep Mr. Bear very, very warm."

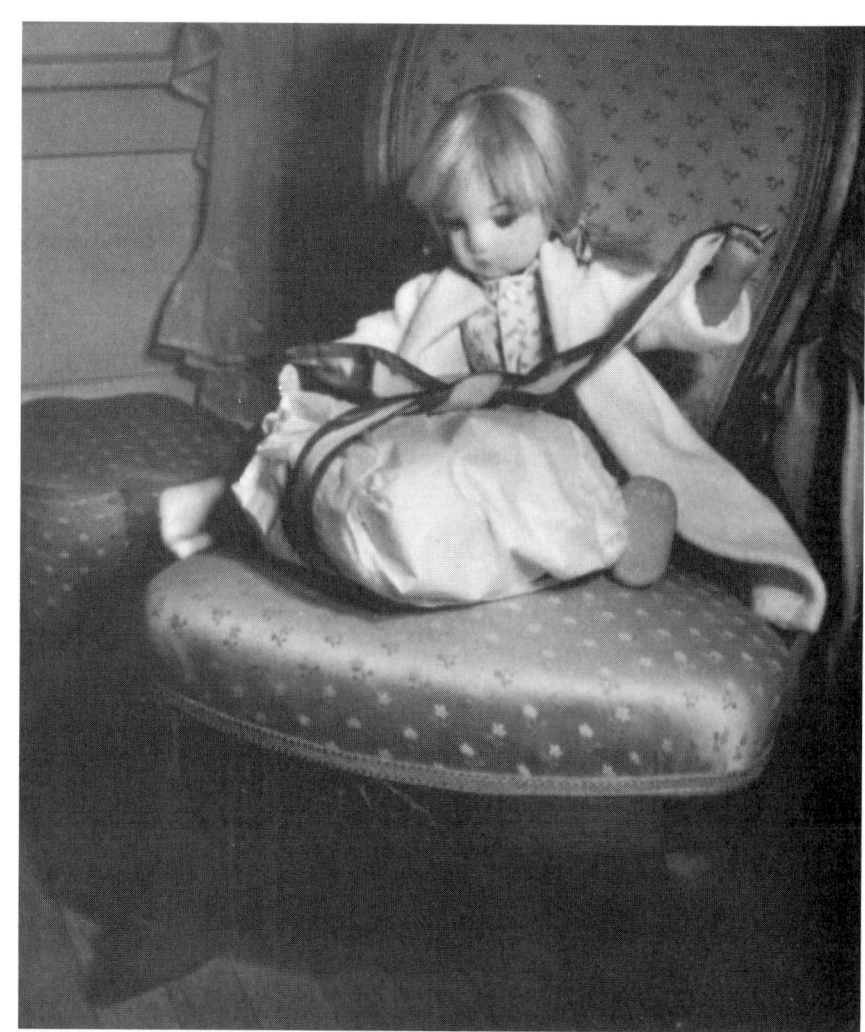

And she wrapped the muffler
in tissue paper and ribbon,

and crept down in the dark
to put it under the tree.

Christmas morning came at last with wonderful surprises
for everyone from everyone.

Edith's favorite present was
a hood of real fur.

Little Bear's was a horn that
made a very loud noise.

Then Edith couldn't wait any longer.
"Open that one, Mr. Bear. It's from me," she said.

"It's a muffler!" exclaimed Mr. Bear.
"I made it myself," said Edith,
"A hand-knit muffler! How warm it looks.
I must try it on right now," said Mr. Bear.

He wrapped it around his neck.

There was rather a lot left over.

He wrapped some more.

Even when he was wrapped from head to foot there
was still some muffler left over.

"I told you so, Edith," said Little Bear, "and look,
there's a hole in it."

"Oh, dear," said Edith.

"That just proves it's handmade. It's the most beautiful muffler in the whole world," declared Mr. Bear.

"It certainly is," agreed Charles and Albert.

But Edith wasn't really comforted.

She thought about Mr. Bear's muffler all day, and even wearing her lovely new hood, indoors and out, didn't comfort her.

Listening to Little Bear blow his horn triumphantly
and shout, "What's too long and full of holes?" didn't
comfort her a bit.

Dressing up for Christmas dinner didn't comfort her.

"You were right all along about Mr. Bear's muffler,

Little Bear," she said sadly.

"Oh, well, Mr. Bear likes it," said Little Bear.

"But I wanted it to be perfect," said Edith.

"Edith, you aren't eating your dinner," said Mr. Bear.
"I'm not hungry. It's because I spoiled your muffler. It's
no good," said Edith.

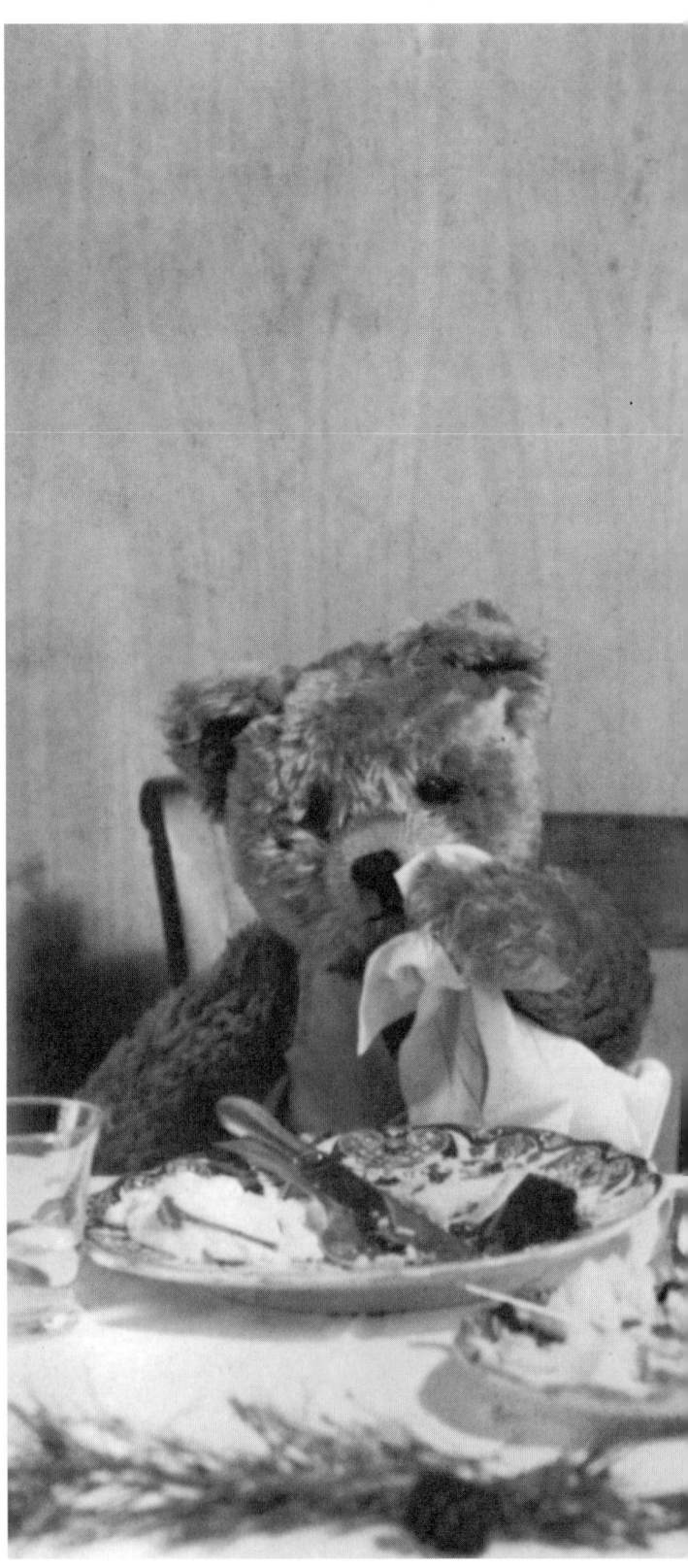

"Why, that muffler's the
nicest present anyone ever
gave me," Mr. Bear said.

"It's a splendid muffler,"
said Albert Bear.

"I wish I had one just like it," declared Charles Bear.

"It's not such a bad muffler," said Little Bear. "You don't have to cry, silly."

So Edith stopped crying, and thought instead, and she had an idea.

When dinner was finished she whispered to Mr. Bear.

"All right," Mr. Bear whispered back, "but I do hate giving up even an inch of my muffler."

"Hey, what are you going to do?" asked Little Bear.

"Fix everything," said Edith.

And that's just what she did.

She took the scissors, and she cut Mr. Bear's

muffler up into three mufflers.

She sewed the ends so they wouldn't ravel.

She even mended the hole.

"Cousin Charles and Cousin Albert," announced Edith,

"I have something for you. Look! Mufflers!"

"Mufflers for us too?" cried Charles and Albert.

"I made them from part of Mr. Bear's, and they're
just the right length," said Edith happily.
"What a muffler!" said Albert.

"What mufflers, you mean!" exclaimed Charles.

"We'll think of you every time we wear them, Edith,"
said Albert.

"And we'll wear them a great deal," said Charles.

They were wearing them proudly when the day came
for Mr. Bear, and Edith, and Little Bear to go home.

"Mr. Bear's muffler wasn't a bit too long," said Edith.

"Not a bit," agreed Little Bear sweetly. "Not a *bit*."

Edith looked at him affectionately.

"*Not for three bears*," added Little Bear.